Books are to be returned on or before
the last date below.

5 OCT 2007

20 SEP 2010

11 DEC 2012

22 MAR 2018

D0533587

LIBREX–

Find out more about
Steve Barlow and Steve Skidmore at
www.the2steves.net

First published in 2007 in Great Britain by
Barrington Stoke Ltd
18 Walker St, Edinburgh, EH3 7LP

www.barringtonstoke.co.uk

ISBN: 978-1-84299-473-3

Printed in Great Britain by Bell & Bain Ltd

Contents

Chapter 1
The Watchers

"Duck under the rotor-blades, if you don't want to lose your head," the CSA agent said.

He held the helicopter door open as Doctor Lee stepped out onto the heli-pad. She bent low to stay under the rotor-blades of the Bell 430 helicopter. As soon as she was clear of the heli-pad, the helicopter rose into the air and banked away.

"This way." The agent led the way down a set of concrete steps. He stopped at a grey steel door. "Behind that door is one of the most top-secret rooms on this planet."

Doctor Lee bit back a giggle. CSA agents were all the same. They just couldn't resist showing off.

The agent pointed at a DNA scanner on the wall. "Place your hand against that. It will check your identity and your security clearance level."

Doctor Lee nodded. "Sure."

She held her hand up to the scanner and waited. The unit flashed green and the door opened.

The agent waved Doctor Lee into the room.

It was dark. The only light came from banks of monitor screens and VDUs. The Doctor could just make out the hunched shapes of operators staring at the screens.

They all wore headsets with earphones and microphones.

She heard someone step out of the darkness.

"Well, well, well. Doctor Lee. Welcome to our humble intelligence-gathering centre. I wish I could say I was happy to see you here."

Doctor Lee knew that voice.

Without turning round, she said, "Hello, Agent Makepeace. I wish I could say I was happy to *be* here." She looked up into the scowling face of the CSA man.

"Don't give me that," snarled Makepeace. "Understand one thing, Doctor. *I'm* going to get Tim Corder. I didn't want you here. He's mine. Stay out of my way."

Doctor Lee shook her head. "The Director sent me here to see how you're getting on. That's all."

"It had better be all," snapped Makepeace. "You were too soft on Corder over that virus stuff. I said so in my report."

"I know. I read your report." Doctor Lee was finding it hard to keep her temper. "Are you still mad about how Corder tricked you?"

Makepeace didn't say anything. He just clenched his fists.

"I've been sent here," the Doctor said, "to look after any computer equipment Corder has with him when you catch him. Or rather, *if* you catch him."

Makepeace gave a bark of laughter. "We're going to get him. We know where he is!"

Chapter 2
The Watched

"Sit down. You're making me nervous."
Tim Corder hit a button on his game
console. His eyes never left the TV screen.

"*I'm* making *you* nervous?" Zeen stopped
pacing around the room. He ran his fingers
through his greasy hair. "Do you want to
know what makes *me* nervous? The CSA has
all kinds of top-secret surveillance
equipment. That makes me nervous. You've

made one of their agents really, really mad at you. *That* makes me nervous. And now, most of that top-secret surveillance equipment is looking for us – that makes me *really* nervous. Maybe it should make you nervous, too."

Tim paused the game and gazed at his friend. Together they had created – and then destroyed – the Doomsday virus. It had been the most destructive virus the world had ever seen.

Tim and Zeen were friends but they were very different. Tim was thin, Zeen was stocky. Tim's hair was dark, Zeen's was fair. Tim was neat and smartly dressed. Zeen wore a dirty T-shirt and shorts. He looked as if he'd just been run over by a truck.

"Chill," Tim told him. "What's the matter with you?"

"What's the matter with me?" Zeen stared at Tim. "Hey, I don't know – maybe I'm fed up of living in this dump." Zeen waved his hands at the peeling walls and the mess of empty burger and pizza boxes.

"Why?"

"Why?" shouted Zeen. "Only because the world's most powerful intelligence agency is breathing down my neck!"

"You're paranoid," Tim said.

"No, paranoid is when you *think* they're out to get you. I *know* they're out to get me. It's only a matter of time."

Tim gave a sigh. "Listen – any surveillance system is only as good as the people who operate it. Makepeace is operating it ..." He grinned. "And Makepeace is an idiot. Relax. He doesn't have a clue where we are."

Chapter 3
The Hunt

"They're right here." Makepeace jabbed a finger at a map of the down-town part of the city. "They're living in a cruddy third-floor apartment. I guess they think they're safe."

Doctor Lee raised her eyebrows. "You seem very sure of yourself."

"I am." Makepeace gave her a grin. "Oh, I admit, we lost Corder for a while. But then we put everything we had into the hunt." He pointed at a bank of screens. "We used surveillance satellites. We had them focus in on every street in the country and use HID software ..."

The Doctor frowned. "What's HID?"

Makepeace was enjoying himself. Last time they'd met, Doctor Lee had been the expert and he'd been asking the questions. But surveillance was what he knew about. This time, he was the expert and she was the school kid.

"HID stands for Human Identification at a Distance."

"What does that do?" asked the Doctor.

"It's bio-metric technology. That means if you were in the database, it could recognise your face from space. It can even recognise the way a person walks! It uses night vision so it can operate 24 hours a day. Impressive, wouldn't you say?"

Doctor Lee shivered. "That's scary."

Makepeace gazed at the screens. "The last generation of spy-birds could read your car number plate from space. The new generation can read the time off your *watch*!"

"Except when it's cloudy," Doctor Lee snapped back. Makepeace scowled. "And yet," the Doctor went on, "even with all your high-tech gadgets, you couldn't find Corder."

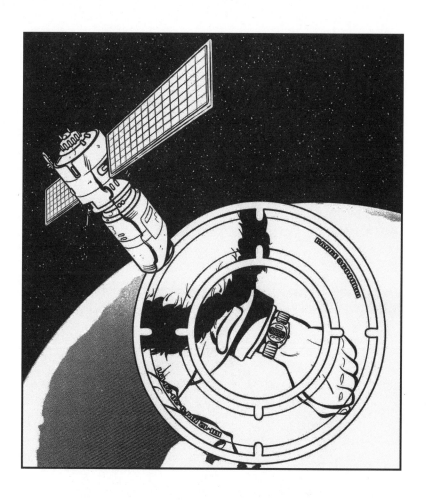

"It took a while, I'll admit." Makepeace
smiled. "But then, Corder made a fatal
mistake. These punk kids think they're so
smart," the agent went on, "but they all
make one mistake, and then – we get 'em."

"Sir." One of the technicians looked up from his screen and gave Makepeace a thumbs-up sign. "The SWAT team just called in. They're ready to go."

Makepeace rubbed his hands together. "Good." He turned to Lee. "You'd better come along for the ride, Doctor – that is, if you want to be in at the kill."

Chapter 4
The Disguise

Zeen was sitting on the sofa biting his nails when Tim stepped in to the apartment and closed the door.

Zeen shot to his feet. "You didn't tell me you were going out! I go to the bathroom for two minutes and when I come out, you're not there! Where did you go?"

"It's OK, Mom," said Tim, "I'm a big boy now, I can cross the street all by myself and tie my own shoelaces and everything." He handed Zeen a burger in a box. "A growing boy's got to eat."

Zeen opened the box and lifted the lid of the bun. "Did you get mustard?" He sniffed. "There are onions in the salad – you know I don't eat onions." He pointed an accusing finger at Tim. "Anyway, don't change the subject. Why did you go out? What if the CSA had spotted you?"

Tim sat down and opened a second burger box. "The CSA won't ever spot me. I always go to a different place and I always pay cash, you know that."

Zeen shook his head. "It's still too risky. They'll spot you one of these days. They'll see you from one of their satellites. Then if they're not sure, the CSA'll check that out with an agent on the ground. They'll get you sooner or later."

Tim shrugged and bit into his burger.

"And what about Remote Piloted Vehicles?" Zeen asked. "I hear they've got RPVs no bigger than a Frisbee. They don't make a noise, and they're controlled by some guy with a palm-top computer." He looked around the room quickly as if there might be a flying camera hovering somewhere.

"You never know who might be watching you," Zeen moaned. "The CSA has cameras that they can fit into a pack of cigarettes – or a jacket button – or even a *tie*."

Tim sighed. "Yeah, yeah – I know. So I when I go out, I change the way I walk. I read a newspaper. I wear shades and a hat – or a hood. I don't look up." He pointed at the box in Zeen's hands. "Quit worrying and eat your burger before it gets cold."

Zeen sat down and nibbled at his burger.

Tim winked at him. "Don't let Makepeace get to you. He can give it his best shot, I'm wise to him. He doesn't stand a chance."

Chapter 5
The Mistake

It was late and the city streets were almost empty as Makepeace drove Doctor Lee towards Tim Corder's hiding place.

Doctor Lee glanced over at Makepeace. "So – are you going to tell me about the big mistake you say Corder made?"

"I'd be happy to," grinned Makepeace. "We watched Corder's house for weeks, but he never showed. He's not *that* stupid."

Doctor Lee almost replied that Tim Corder wasn't stupid at all, but she stayed silent.

"So, we waited until there was no one at home." Agent Makepeace sounded very pleased with himself. "We went in and found Corder's personal possessions. Then we replaced them with items that looked identical."

"I hope you had a search warrant," snapped Doctor Lee.

Makepeace gave her a disgusted look. "What are you moaning about? We replaced everything, but the stuff we left contained RFID tags."

Doctor Lee nodded. "Radio Frequency Identification – I've heard of that."

"That's right." Makepeace looked annoyed that he didn't have to explain what RFID was. "Anyway, we planted electronic bugs that would let us know everywhere that Corder went. Our systems would show us wherever he was. The bugs were in Corder's things if he was dumb enough to come get them. And he *was* dumb enough." Makepeace laughed.

Doctor Lee was startled. "He came and got his things himself?"

Makepeace shook his head angrily. "Of course not – if he'd done that, we'd have jumped him there and then. No, someone else came and collected Corder's stuff three days ago. Maybe it was Zeen, that guy he works with."

"And you didn't arrest the person who collected the stuff?"

Makepeace gave a nasty grin. "Not on your life. Sure, we want Zeen, too – but Corder's the one we're really after. We wanted the stuff to get to him. Anyhow, we figured that when we caught Corder, we'd get Zeen as well."

"A bird in the hand is worth two in the bush," muttered Doctor Lee.

"Did you say something?" asked Makepeace.

"It's not important," said Doctor Lee.

"Anyhow," the agent went on, "we tracked the bugged items. They stopped moving at a downtown apartment block. That's where we're going now."

Doctor Lee said nothing. She didn't trust herself to speak. Makepeace was getting on her nerves. He was so pleased with himself.

Makepeace was still gloating. "The tags stopped moving around because Corder had got them. He's wearing them. He's sending out radio waves like a phone mast, and he doesn't know! He's ours!"

Chapter 6
The Silence

"What are you doing?"

Zeen gave Tim a sulky look. "I'm writing an email to my brother."

"No, you're not," said Tim. "We agreed – no electronic communication. No phone calls, no faxes, no texts. Anything that can be intercepted by the CSA will bring them down on us like a ton of bricks. And they can intercept emails, remember?"

"I'm not stupid," snapped Zeen. "I'm going to encrypt it."

"No good. The CSA operators can always decode encrypted emails. They have backdoor passwords. There's no point in putting something into code when the bad guys can read the code."

Zeen gazed at the screen of his laptop and said nothing.

"That's why we have to be careful," Tim told him. "The CSA checks credit and debit card histories, so we don't use plastic to buy stuff. They check gas and electricity bills, so we only stay in places where the apartment rent covers those bills too. And where the landlord doesn't ask too many questions. That's why we're here." He waved a hand at the grotty apartment. "Also, the CSA checks all bus and train tickets, so we cadge lifts, or travel under false names and cover our tracks. They also check medical records ..."

"So we can't get sick," said Zeen. He switched off his laptop and closed the case. "OK, I'll write my brother a letter."

Tim shook his head. "The CSA has scanners that can read letters without even opening the envelopes. Sorry, no letters, no emails. It's the only way to stay safe. We'll find a way to contact your brother later."

Scowling, Zeen said, "If there *is* a later."

Chapter 7
The Hunters

Makepeace peered round the corner at the apartment block on the other side of the street. Only two of the windows on the third floor were lit. The rest were dark. The agent gave a satisfied grunt. "No one watching. OK, let's go."

He took Doctor Lee by the arm and strode along the pavement. The Doctor had to run to keep up. Before she had a chance to protest, Agent Makepeace stopped beside a parked van. A sign on its side said **Cutie Cupcakes**.

Doctor Lee glared at the agent. "If you're that desperate for a cupcake, we could have stopped off at a gas station on the way here."

In the darkness, she saw a flash of perfect white teeth as Makepeace grinned. "The only cupcakes in there are my surveillance crew," he said. "And believe me, they ain't cute." He took a key from his pocket, checked that the street was clear, opened the back door of the van and pushed Doctor Lee inside.

The inside of the van was crammed with electronics and LCD screens watched by three CSA operators. "Our mobile VSU," Makepeace told Doctor Lee. "You've heard of Video Surveillance Units?"

Lee nodded.

Makepeace pointed to the bank of screens. "Each screen monitors a spy camera." He pointed to another rack of instruments. "Hard disc recorders linked to uni-directional microphones. Those babies can pick up conversations at a distance of 100 metres, as long as it's in a line-of-sight."

Doctor Lee took a set of headphones and listened to one earpiece. "I can hear voices," she said after a while, "but I can't make out what they're saying."

Makepeace shrugged. "That's because there are trees between us and Corder's apartment – the microphones don't like trees. No matter." He pointed at a screen showing the outline of a building. On the third floor of the outline, four coloured dots glowed. Makepeace nodded grimly. "They're in there, all right." He pointed to the screen. "There are four RFID tags – one in Corder's mobile phone, one in his belt buckle. The others are in an MP3 player, and his wristwatch."

Doctor Lee thought about this. "The *tags* are there ... but how do you know Corder's wearing them?"

Makepeace gave her a smug grin. "Because of the wristwatch. We know Corder's wearing the wristwatch because *that* tag shows up the heartbeat of the person who's wearing it." He pointed at the blinking dot labelled 'watch'.

The operator at the screen looked up. "The guy sure seems excited about something," he grinned. "His heartbeat's racing."

Makepeace gave a shrug. "Maybe he's watching a football game on TV. Who cares? He's caught like a rat in a trap."

"Wait!" The operator watched as the blinking dot began to crawl across the screen. "He's on the move."

Chapter 8
The Hunted

Tim's thumbs danced over the buttons of his console. He watched the game playing on the TV screen with fierce intensity.

Zeen was standing at the window, peering through a gap in the curtains. He said, "Hey."

Tim took no notice. Zeen said, "Hey," again, a little louder this time.

Tim's eyes never left the screen. "Will you shut up? I'm trying to beat my all-time best score."

Zeen went on talking. "There's a delivery van out there. It hasn't moved for hours. What do you suppose that means?"

"It means the delivery guy has parked it there for the night." Tim swore as he failed to duck a Zargon Mind Slave with a laser sword. The enemy took 40 per cent of his health with one stroke before Tim's power-blaster blew it to atoms. "Will you shut up? How am I supposed to concentrate?"

"That van could be a Video Surveillance Unit." Zeen said. "It could have the whole block covered by a dedicated surveillance satellite. There could be guys inside the van watching hidden movement-activated cameras and RPVs."

"Or it could be a delivery van." Tim groaned as his game character dropped through a hidden trap-door and fell into a pit of snakes. "Now look what you did! I was three hundred points short." Tim glared at the *GAME OVER* sign and threw his controller onto the sofa in disgust. He checked his watch. "I'm out of toothpaste. I'm going out to the late shop."

Chapter 9
The Trace

Makepeace and Doctor Lee peered over the operator's shoulder as the blinking dot of the watch tag moved through the apartment block.

The operator followed the dot's movement. "Corder is going out of the back door – along the alley – hold it!" He stared at the screen. "This is crazy. It looks like there's a change in his vertical position."

Doctor Lee said, "What does that mean?"

Makepeace looked puzzled. "It means he's going up." He gave the operator a hard look. "You sure about that?"

The operator nodded unhappily. "Yes, sir – I know it sounds crazy but he seems to be on a wall ..." The operator watched as the blinking dot continued to move up. "And now he's on the roof."

"On the roof?" Makepeace stared at the screen. "Who does this guy think he is – Santa Claus? What are the other tags doing?"

The operator shrugged. "Nothing – they're still in the apartment."

Makepeace gave a snarl and snatched a microphone from the shelf in front of the screen. "All stations," he barked, "eyes up!

Subject is on the roof of the next building south – I need visual confirmation." He glared at the operators.

The second operator said, "No confirmation from satellite."

Makepeace turned to the third operator. "How about the RPVs?"

The third operator shook his head. Makepeace swore.

Reports started to come in from watchers on the ground. They were all negative. No one could see where Corder was.

"Now listen up!" Makepeace gripped the microphone so hard his knuckles shone white. "We aren't dealing with the Invisible Man here. Find him!"

Slowly, Doctor Lee said, "OK, I can see he
might go out wearing his watch and not
take his mobile phone or his MP3 player.
But what happened to the tag on his belt?
Why would he go out without his *trousers*?"

"Maybe he's wearing jogging pants today and he doesn't need a belt," snapped Makepeace. "How the hell would I know?"

"Wait!" The operator watching the tags gave a sigh of relief. "He's turned back. It looks like he's going back to the apartment. Yes." The operator leaned back and put his hands over his eyes.

But Makepeace was still as tense as a coiled spring. "I'm up to here with this punk taking me for a sucker. Enough pussy-footing around. Call the SWAT team – we're going in!"

Chapter 10
The Raid

From outside the apartment there was a thunder of feet and a roar of voices. Then the door was smashed in and men burst into the room. They were wearing flak jackets and riot helmets, and carrying torches and machine pistols. They took up firing positions and looked around.

Makepeace strode in behind them. He stopped in the centre of the room. His jaw dropped.

The apartment was empty except for a TV with a DVD player and a clock-radio sitting on top of it. Across the room was a music centre and an old sofa. Lying on the sofa and staring at the intruders was a cat. It was wearing a watch round its neck.

Makepeace said, "What in the world ...?"

Doctor Lee had come in behind him. She was watching the TV. It was showing a recording of Tim Corder and another boy, who kept his back to the camera. They were playing *Pat-a-Cake, Pat-a-Cake, Baker's Man*.

The head of the SWAT spoke into a microphone that was fixed to his jacket. "Target secure. Subjects *not*, repeat *not*, at this location. Stand down."

He gave Makepeace a scornful look. "Nice operation, Agent. Next time you need a SWAT team to help you arrest a pussy cat, be sure and let us know." He led his men out of the door. Their laughter drifted back into the room.

Doctor Lee pointed at the cat. "No wonder you were picking up a racing heartbeat. A cat's heart beats twice as fast as a human's." She grinned. "And no wonder your agents didn't see it on the roof."

Makepeace stared at nothing for a moment. Then he looked down. At his feet was an empty steel cat-bowl. Makepeace swore and kicked the bowl across the apartment.

The TV flickered. Doctor Lee watched it for a moment. Then she said, "Agent Makepeace, have you seen what's on TV?"

"Who the hell cares?"

"I really think you should look at this."

Makepeace stopped kicking things. "So what *is* on TV?"

"You are."

Chapter 11
The Farewell

Makepeace stared at the TV. His own face, mouth open and red with rage, stared back at him.

"I guess the camera must be in the clock-radio," said Doctor Lee helpfully. Makepeace snarled and reached for the small device. But before he could rip it to bits, the TV flickered again. This time Tim's face was on the screen. "Agent Makepeace," he said with a smile, "how are you doing? Doctor Lee, good to see you again!"

The Doctor stared at the screen. "Hello, Tim. Can you hear us?"

"Sure thing. I rigged the loudspeakers of the music centre to work as microphones. It's easy when you know how. I've been watching and listening to everything that's been going on." He gave the angry Makepeace a wink. "Good raid, better than a movie."

The agent's face was set in an animal snarl. "Where are you, you little creep?"

"Wouldn't you like to know?" said Tim. "I'll tell you one thing – I'm not where you are, or anywhere within 500 miles of it."

Makepeace struggled to stay cool. "Keep watching your back, wise guy. I'll get you in the end. This is a mouse-hunt. I'm the cat, and you're the mouse."

Tim nodded. "You may be right, Agent. Maybe I am a mouse. But I'm a smart mouse and you're a dumb cat."

Makepeace opened and closed his mouth twice. Then he turned and stormed out of the apartment in a rage.

"Doctor Lee?"

Lee turned back to the TV. "Yes, Tim?"

"Listen, Doc, I don't want to put you to any trouble, but could you look after my cat?"

Doctor Lee looked down at the cat on the sofa. The cat looked right back up at her, and said, "Miaow?"

"I reckoned it would take Makepeace two days to find the apartment. In fact it took him three. I only left food for two days, so maybe the cat's getting hungry. Her name's Cleo." Tim checked his watch. "Hey, listen, Doc, I've got to run before Makepeace cools down enough to think about tracing this

transmission. He's bugged me enough! See you around. Wave goodbye to the Doctor, Zeen."

A hand appeared at the edge of the screen and waved. Then the TV went blank.

Doctor Lee thought for a moment. Then she picked up Cleo and took the watch off the cat's neck. She put the watch on the sofa and left the apartment.

The street was already empty. The SWAT team had left. The VSU van had gone.

Doctor Lee smiled to herself. She tucked the cat firmly under her arm, and walked off into the night.

Glossary

BIOMETRIC TECHNOLOGY

Technology that measures and works out how to identify someone. For example, a computer might use someone's fingerprints, or an eye scan. More advanced equipment can recognize a person from the way he or she walks.

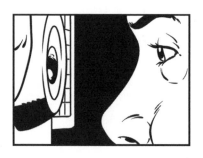

DNA

The molecule in the body that holds the genetic information for a person. Everyone has different DNA.

ENCRYPTION

To turn computer data into something no one can read unless they know the code.

HACKER

A person who tries to break through a computer or network security system.

HID

Abbreviation for Human Identification at a Distance. Cameras take an image of a person and feed it into a computer. The computer examines how the person looks and walks. It checks these results on a database so as to identify that person.

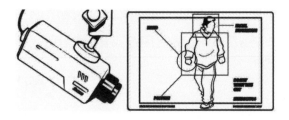

LCD

Abbreviation for Liquid Crystal Display. LCD screens are used in most computers and other digital instruments.

MOVEMENT-ACTIVATED CAMERA

A camera that only switches on when someone or something moves nearby.

RFID

Abbreviation for Radio Frequency Identification. An RFID tag is a small object that can be attached to a person or thing to show its location by using radio waves.

There are many different types of RFID tags. The tags that make the alarm go off in clothes shops are RFID tags. In surveillance work, these tags are called "bugs".

RPV

Abbreviation for Remote Piloted Vehicle. Also sometimes known as UAV (Unmanned Aerial Vehicle). These are remote-controlled aircraft. They are sometimes piloted from the ground or controlled automatically by a computer.

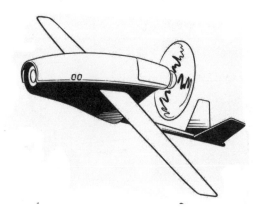

SATELLITE

This term is mostly used for man-made objects that orbit the Earth. There are many different types of satellites for doing different things. Some are for surveillance and others carry TV signals, phone messages and emails.

SURVEILLANCE

Watching a person or group of people who are suspected of doing something illegal.

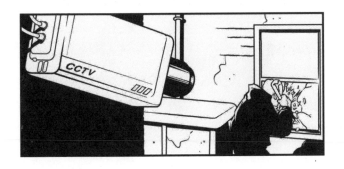

SWAT

Abbreviation of Special Weapons and Tactics. These are special police units trained to perform dangerous operations. Also known as Tactical Firearms Units or Armed Response Units.

UNI-DIRECTIONAL MICROPHONES

Microphones that pick up sounds from one direction. They can pick up people talking softly from over 100 metres away but only if there are no objects in between the microphone and the people talking.

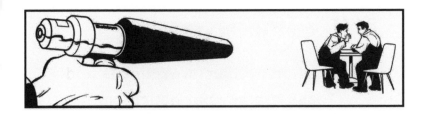

VDU

Abbreviation for Visual Display Unit, a monitor that displays images from a computer.

AUTHOR FACT FILE

If you could invent any gadget in the world, what would it be?
Barlow: A rewind switch for life. So that if I say anything I regret, or drop something valuable, I could press the switch and life would rewind until it hadn't happened. I'd call it Instant Replay.
Skidmore: A time travel machine. I'd call it 'a time travel machine' (it does what it says on the machine!).

Tell us some TOP SECRET info about you:
Barlow: I'm a Formula 1 racing driver, a champion skier, a world class violin player and a black belt in karate. All this is so top secret that none of my friends know anything about it and if you tried to tell them, they wouldn't believe you.
Skidmore: If I did that, it wouldn't be top secret!

If you could listen in to someone's conversation in secret, who would it be and why?
Barlow: Any politician, to see if they are lying ALL the time.
Skidmore: Kids TV presenters. They have to pretend to be so matey on screen, but I bet they all hate each other really.

If you could own any gadget in the world, what would it be?
Barlow: A "Star Wars" light saber – not a tacky plastic one, a proper one with an energy blade that goes "verzoooing!"

ILLUSTRATOR FACT FILE

What's you favourite satellite show?
Boston Legal, Bones or Battlestar Galactica – all
the Bs!

Tell us some TOP SECRET info about you:
I once paraded around the centre of Oxford in a
badger costume!

**If you could listen in to someone's conversation in
secret, who would it be and why?**
I wouldn't. Ignorance is bliss.

**If you were on the run from the CSA, where would
you hide?**
In the centre of Oxford in a badger costume (no one
can recognise you)!

**If you could own any gadget in the world, what would
it be?**
I'd love a digital SLR (a very hi-tech cutting edge
camera). *So* cool.

**If you could invent any gadget in the world,
what would it be?**
A gadget to get rid of all those annoying channel
adverts you get on satellite TV channels.

Barrington Stoke would like to thank all its readers for commenting on the manuscript before publication and in particular:

Megan Austin

Stephanie Bowen

Andrew Brodie

Ellie Campbell

Michael Hughes

Lisa Kerr

Ross McColgan

Claire McKay

Jack McWilliams

James Siddle

James Smith

Margaret Smith

Julie Sutherland

Become a Consultant!

Would you like to give us feedback on our titles before they are published? Contact us at the email address below – we'd love to hear from you!

info@barringtonstoke.co.uk
www.barringtonstoke.co.uk